My book of
bedtime
rhymes

Illustrated by MARGARET CHAMBERLAIN

Ladybird Books

Come to the window, my baby, with me,
And look at the stars that shine on the sea!
There are two little stars that play at bo-peep
With two little fish far down in the deep;
And two little frogs cry, "Neap, neap, neap,
I see a dear baby that should be asleep."

Star light, star bright,
First star I see tonight,
I wish I may,
I wish I might,
Have the wish
I wish tonight.

Twinkle, twinkle, little star,
How I wonder what you are!
Up above the world so high,
Like a diamond in the sky.

I see the moon,
And the moon sees me.
God bless the moon,
And God bless me.

The Man in the Moon looked out of the moon,
And this is what he said:
"Now that I'm getting up, it's time
All children went to bed."

Early to bed and early to rise
Makes a man healthy, wealthy, and wise.

How many miles to Babylon?
Threescore miles and ten.
Can I get there by candlelight?
Yes, and back again.
If your heels are nimble and light,
You may get there by candlelight.

Bossy-cow, bossy-cow, where do you lie?
In the green meadows, under the sky.

Billy-horse, billy-horse, where do you lie?
Out in the stable, with nobody nigh.

Birdies bright, birdies bright, where do you lie?
Up in the treetops, ever so high!

Baby dear, baby dear, where do you lie?
In my warm cradle, with Mother close by.

Golden slumbers kiss your eyes,
Smiles awake you when you rise.
Sleep, pretty baby, do not cry,
And I will sing a lullaby:
Rock them, rock them, lullaby.

Rock-a-bye, baby, in the treetop!
When the wind blows, the cradle will rock.
When the bough breaks, the cradle will fall,
And down will come baby, cradle, and all.

If my boy sleeps quietly,
He shall see the busy bee,
When it has made its honey fine,
Dancing in the bright sunshine.
If my boy will slumber,
Angels without number
Will draw near, so fair and bright,
For they only come at night.

Rock-a-bye, baby, thy cradle is green;
Father's a nobleman, Mother's a queen;
And Betty's a lady, and wears a gold ring;
And Johnny's a drummer, and drums for the king.

Hush, little baby, don't say a word,
Papa's going to buy you a mockingbird.
If that mockingbird won't sing,
Papa's going to buy you a diamond ring.
If that diamond ring turns brass,
Papa's going to buy you a looking glass.
If that looking glass gets broke,
Papa's going to buy you a billy goat.
If that billy goat won't pull,
Papa's going to buy you a cart and bull.
If that cart and bull fall down,
You'll still be the sweetest little baby in town!

Wee Willie Winkie runs through the town,
Upstairs and downstairs, in his nightgown;
Rapping at the window, crying through the lock,
"Are the children in their beds?
For now it's eight o'clock."

Diddle, diddle, dumpling, my son John,
Went to bed with his trousers on;
One shoe off, and one shoe on;
Diddle, diddle, dumpling, my son John.

"To bed! To bed!" says Sleepyhead;
"Let's stay awhile," says Slow;
"Put on the pan," says Greedy Sam,
"Let's sup before we go."

A glass of milk and a slice of bread,
And then good night, we must go to bed.

Up the wooden hill
To Bedfordshire,
Down Sheet Lane
To Blanket Fair.

And now, good night, our play is done,
Farewell to each and every one.